P9-DFL-419

VIKING   Published   by   Penguin   Group

Penguin Young Readers Group, 345 Hudson Street, New York, New

York 10014, U.S.A. • Penguin Group (Canada), 90 Eglinton Avenue East, Suite 700,

Toronto, Ontario, Canada M4P 2Y3 (a division of Pearson Penguin Canada Inc.)

Penguin Books Ltd, 80 Strand, London WC2R 0RL, England • Penguin Ireland, 25 St Stephen's Green,

Dublin 2, Ireland (a division of Penguin Books Ltd) • Penguin Group (Australia), 250 Camberwell Road,

Camberwell, Victoria 3124, Australia (a division of Pearson Australia Group Pty Ltd) • Penguin Books

India Pvt Ltd, 11 Community Centre, Panchsheel Park, New Delhi – 110 017, India • Penguin Group (NZ), Cnr

Airborne and Rosedale Roads, Albany, Auckland 1310, New Zealand (a division of Pearson New Zealand Ltd)

Penguin Books (South Africa) (Pty) Ltd, 24 Sturdee Avenue, Rosebank, Johannesburg 2196, South Africa •

Penguin Books Ltd, Registered Offices: 80 Strand, London WC2R 0RL, England • First published in

2006 by Viking, a division of Penguin Young Readers Group • Manufactured in China •

Copyright © Peter Kuper, 2006   All rights reserved   Book Design by Peter Kuper

and Jim Hoover   Set in Futura Condensed, Bagheera, and Base Nine

1   3   5   7   9   10   8   6   4   2

LIBRARY OF CONGRESS CATALOGING-IN-PUBLICATION DATA   Kuper, Peter, date–   Theo and the blue note / by Peter Kuper   p. cm.   Summary: Theo the cat has learned to play only one blue note on his saxophone, but when a magical rocket ship carries him to the moon, he joins Charlie Parker, Nat King Cobra, Duck Ellington, and other great jazz musicians in a jam session.   ISBN 0-670-06137-9 (hardcover)   [1. Musicians–Fiction. 2. Jazz–Fiction. 3. Space flight to the moon–Fiction. 4. Cats–Fiction. 5. Animals–Fiction.]   I. Title.   PZ7.K9497The 2006   [E]–dc22   2005035354

So, what's a BLUE NOTE?

It's a flatted note, especially the third or seventh note

of a scale. To hear it, just listen to jazz music.

FOR EMILY,
THE HEPPEST CAT I KNOW

Stencils, spray paint, watercolors, colored pencils, and collage were used to play this song.

My beret is off to
Jules Feiffer, Emily Russell,
Jim Rasenberger, Julie Grau, Betty Russell,
John Thomas, Ryan Inzana, Joy Peskin,
Jim Hoover, Regina Hayes, Denise Cronin,
Cathy Young, Eve Grandt, Rocky Maffit,
Garin Thomas, Kevin Pyle,
Scott Cunningham,
Thelonious Monk,
Lionel Hampton,
Chico O'Farrill,
Ella Fitzgerald,
Nat King Cole,
Duke Ellington,
Charlie Parker,
Billie Holiday,
Sonny Rollins,
Miles Davis,
Chet Baker,
and
Max Roach.

THEO loved the saxophone
so much he practiced **DAY** **AND**

Mastering the sax seemed as far out of Theo's reach as the rising moon.

He was feeling
KIND OF BLUE
when a flash of gold
caught his eye. . . .

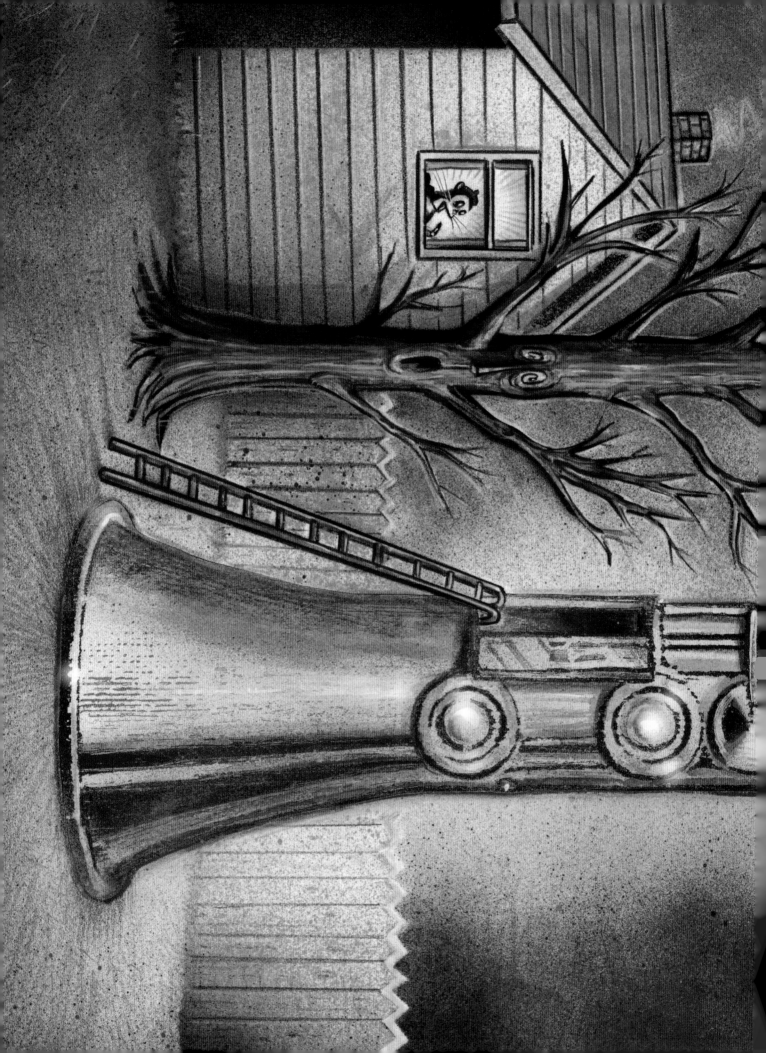

Was that a gleaming yellow
rocket ship standing in the
backyard?

Theo quickly climbed

DOWN

the ladder
to the rocket's door . . .

UP

the tree
outside
his window . . . **THEN**

Inside the ship was
a magnificent jukebox
filled with songs by
musicians Theo loved.

He couldn't
resist ...

There was a tickle of piano
keys, a rat-a-tat of drums,
a boom-boom of bass,
a blast of trumpets,
and . . .

As the
music ended,
so did the
trip. . . .

It was awfully quiet on the moon, so Theo played his sax to keep from getting lonely.

He climbed a hill to get a better look around . . .

. . . and his heart skipped a beat.

Another
spacecraft?

And was that
music
Theo heard?

It was coming from inside, beyond those **GIANT STEPS!**

Theo couldn't believe his eyes!

CHIMP BAKER
on guitar

LIONEL HAMSTER
on xylophone

was a big band of **FAMOUS MUSICIANS!**

**Suddenly,
Duck Ellington
flapped his wings....**

STOP! EVERYONE, STOP!

"The song's just not right.
It's got the RED note, the GREEN,
the YELLOW, the PURPLE,
the ORANGE, the BROWN,
and even
the PINK note . . .

but something's
still missing."

The
BLUE NOTE,
of course!

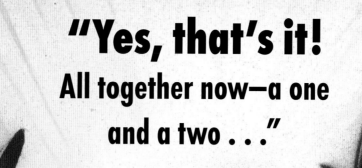

Blasting **COOL** jazz with a **HOT** beat, the Apollo flew to earth

and Theo pointed out his

HOUSE

As the band shouted their good nights, Duck promised they'd all play together again the next full moon.

Theo listened until the music faded, picturing playing all those colorful notes....

They were no farther from his reach than the moon!

SYRENIUS H. BO... ...RY
3 4014 142
8/18